MORNINGS ARE NEVER THE BEST OF TIMES FOR ME. I LIKE TO BOOT UP SLOWLY; TAKE A LEISURELY APPROACH; REALLY GET MY CIRCUITS IN GEAR FOR THE DAY AHEAD.

ACTUALLY, BY THE TIME I WAKE UP, IT'S MORE ACCURATE TO SAY THE *NIGHT* AHEAD. THE AGENCY DOES MOST OF ITS WORK AT NIGHT ANYWAY.

THE AGENCY. THAT'S ROBOT CITY CONFIDENTIAL INVESTIGATIONS--ROBOT CITY'S PREMIER PRIVATE DETECTIVE AGENCY, IF I DO SAY SO MYSELF.

WE TAKE GREAT PRIDE IN OUR WORK...

HELPING CLIENTS WITH WHATEVER LITTLE DIFFICULTIES THEY MIGHT HAVE.

YUP. I'M AN AGENCY ROBOT...

A CONFIDENTIAL ROBOT RIGHT DOWN TO MY RIVETS.

THE AGENCY CONSISTS OF ME; MIKE STONE, MY PARTNER; AND ELAINE, OUR SECRETARY.

WE MET BACK WHEN WE WORKED FOR THE ROBOT CITY POLICE DEPARTMENT.
WE LIKE TO THINK THAT OUR ORGANISATION IS QUICK TO REACT AND PROFESSIONAL.
WE HAVE HONED OURSELVES INTO THE SHARPEST, MOST ASTUTE, MOST RELIABLE PRIVATE INVESTIGATORS IN ROBOT CITY. AT LEAST, THAT'S WHAT WE LIKE TO THINK!
ROBOT CITY CONFIDENTIAL
INVESTIGATIONS
I NEED A BIG CUP OF COFFEE TO GET GOING TODAY.
ME TOO. ARE YOU BUYING?
I THOUGHT IT WAS YOUR TURN.
IT'S NOT MINE. MIKE, IT MUST BE YOUR TURN.
UH--I'VE LEFT MY WALLET AT HOME. COFFEE'S OFF TODAY!

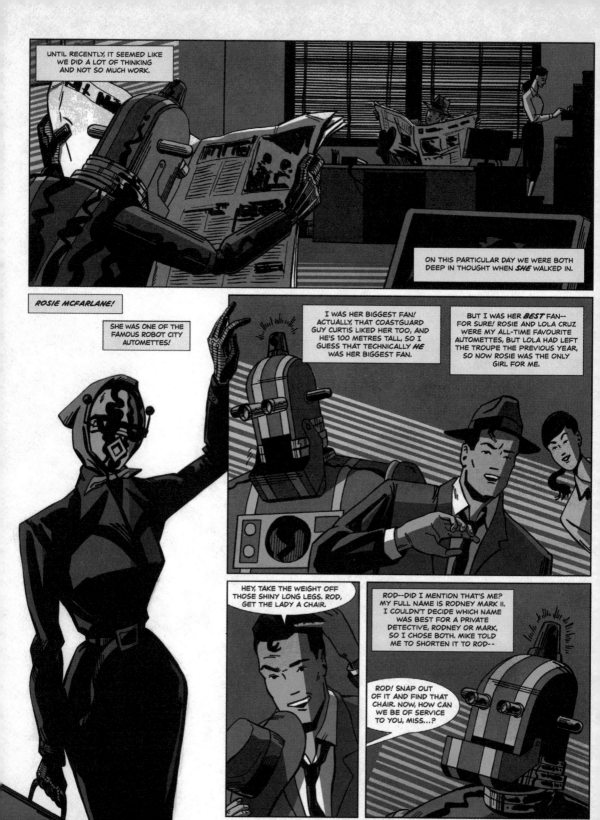

GOOD GRIEF! MY JAW HIT THE FLOOR. LITERALLY.

I COULDN'T BELIEVE MY EYES.

IT WAS THE ONE THING THAT HAUNTS MY DREAMS; THE ONE THING THAT EVERY ROBOT DREADS; THE TERROR WHOSE NAME WE DARE NOT SPEAK... *RUST!*

THE AUTOMETTES WERE RUSTING, AND THEY'D COME TO US FOR HELP! THINGS HAD JUST GOT SERIOUS.

ROSIE, THINGS HAVE JUST GOT SERIOUS. IT'S IMPORTANT THAT YOU TELL US EVERYTHING YOU KNOW.

WHO DID THIS TO YOU? WE HAVE TO FIND OUT BEFORE THE RUST SPREADS TO EVERY ROBOT IN THE CITY!

WELL, I CAN'T SAY FOR SURE WHAT CAUSED IT, BUT TWO MONTHS AGO THE AUTOMETTES WERE APPROACHED BY A ROBOT WITH A NEW-FORMULA BODY WAX. HE OFFERED IT TO US FOR FREE, AND IT WAS SO GOOD.

I'LL SAY! I MEAN, UH, WHAT A FANTASTIC, UH, PRODUCT.

IT WAS BETTER THAN ANYTHING WE'D EVER USED BEFORE. IT MADE US LOOK SHINY AND BRAND NEW.

BUT NOW, LOOK! WE'RE RUSTING!

WE TRIED TO FIND THE GUY WHO SOLD US THIS STUFF, BUT HE'S DISAPPEARED.

SO MAYBE THE RUST IS A SIDE EFFECT OF THE BODY WAX?

GOOD THINKING, ROD. LET'S GET ON IT. WE HAVE TO FIND THIS WAX SUPPLIER BEFORE HE INFECTS ANY OTHER ROBOTS.

COME INTO MY OFFICE AND CLOSE THE DOOR. I DON'T WANT ANYONE ELSE HEARING ABOUT THIS.

I DON'T KNOW IF YOU KNEW, BUT MY WIFE, VICTORIA, USED TO DANCE WITH THE AUTOMETTES.

YOU'RE MARRIED TO A ROBOT?

NO, ROD, SHE'S A HUMAN. DON'T FORGET, THE AUTOMETTES ARE MADE UP OF BOTH ROBOT AND HUMAN DANCERS.

ANYWAY, ROSIE MCFARLANE CAME TO SEE VICTORIA BECAUSE SHE KNEW I WAS IN THE RCPD.

THE THING IS, RUST IS KIND OF A TOUCHY SUBJECT IN THIS TOWN.

I'LL SAY. JUST THE MENTION OF IT MADE MY CIRCUITS CRAWL.

I CAN'T PUT ANY RCPD DETECTIVES ON THIS WITHOUT STARTING A PANIC. SO I THOUGHT, WHO BETTER THAN TWO OF MY BEST FORMER OFFICERS TO TAKE ON THE CASE?

GREAT! AND WILL WE BE WORKING WITH THEM?

ROD, ARE YOU SURE YOU PLUGGED IN YOUR MEMORY CHIP TODAY? YOU GUYS *DID* USED TO BE TWO OF RCPD'S FINEST.

YOU NAILED EVERY SINGLE ONE OF YOUR CASES. WELL, APART FROM THE MAXWELL WEST CASE, BUT WE'RE NOT MIRACLE WORKERS. YOU GUYS ARE PROS!

WELL, THERE YOU GO. IT WAS OFFICIAL--WE WERE GOOD. SO WHY DIDN'T LIEUTENANT COLE EVER TELL US THAT WHEN WE WORKED FOR HIM?

SO, LIEUTENANT, HAVE YOU GOT ANY LEADS TO GET US STARTED ON THIS LITTLE JOB FOR THE AUTOMETTES?

YES I HAVE, BUT I'VE GOT TO KNOW THAT YOU'LL TREAT ALL THIS CONFIDENTIALLY.

I'M A CONFIDENTIAL MAN.

AND I'M A CONFIDENTIAL ROBOT.

ALL RIGHT. THE ONE SUSPECT WE HAVE IS A MUSICIAN. HIS NAME IS SLIM MELROSE. HE'S A SAXOPHONE-PLAYING ROBOT FROM DRAGON CITY.

HE GOT A SPOT AT ROBOT CITY MUSIC HALL TO PLAY A NUMBER WITH THE AUTOMETTES. IT WAS HIS BIG CHANCE, AND HE BLEW IT.

SLIM WAS SO BAD THAT HE GOT BOOED OFF STAGE. APPARENTLY HE WAS VERY CUT UP ABOUT IT, AND THE RUMOUR IS HE BLAMES THE AUTOMETTES FOR RUINING HIS CHANCE.

CAN WE FIND HIM AT ROBOT CITY MUSIC HALL?

NO. HE WAS FIRED. SOME ILLEGALLY DOWNLOADED ROBOT MUSIC SOFTWARE WAS FOUND IN HIS DRESSING ROOM.

IT ALSO TURNED OUT HE HADN'T PAID HIS UNION FEES, SO THE MANAGEMENT GOT RID OF HIM AS QUICKLY AS THEY COULD.

BUT THIS IS WHERE HE WORKS NOW--CLUB TIN CAN--AND THIS IS THE ADDRESS FOR HIS APARTMENT. HE HAPPENS TO BE OUT AT THE CLUB EVERY DAY FROM FIVE IN THE EVENING.

LIEUTENANT COLE! SURELY YOU'RE NOT SUGGESTING A LITTLE BIT OF BREAKING AND ENTERING? WOULDN'T THAT BE ILLEGAL?

WE NEED TO GET DOWN TO CLUB TIN CAN TONIGHT. WE'VE GOT TO FIND MELROSE BEFORE THE LUNATIC MANAGES TO INFECT ANY MORE ROBOTS!

CAN WE USE THE STAIRS?

OH, NO!

NO, ROD. LET'S REMAIN INCONSPICUOUS. IT'S OUT THE WAY WE CAME IN.

LATER THAT NIGHT. CLUB TIN CAN.

AT THE AGENCY WE PRIDE OURSELVES ON OUR AMAZING ABILITY TO BLEND IN TO ANY LOCATION.

CLUB TIN CAN

MUSIC

CLUB TIN CAN

DANCING

CLUB TIN CAN

THAT EVENING YOU WOULD HAVE THOUGHT THAT MIKE, ELAINE AND I WERE JUST NORMAL ROBOT CITY CITIZENS OUT FOR A NIGHT OF FUN.

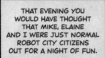

OUR SUSPECT, SLIM MELROSE, WAS PLAYING A SAXOPHONE SOLO, AND I HAVE TO ADMIT HE WAS PRETTY GOOD... FOR A DRAGON CITY ROBOT, ANYWAY.

THE NEXT MORNING.

POLICE WERE CALLED TO THE CITY CENTRE LAST NIGHT TO BREAK UP A RIOT AT CLUB TIN CAN. RUMOURS THAT IT WAS TRIGGERED BY FEARS OF A *RUST* OUTBREAK WERE LAUGHED OFF BY THE MAYOR THIS MORNING.

AND FINALLY, RO-BALL, AND NEWS OF A BIG SIGNING FOR THE ROBOT CITY DYNAMOS TODAY. LOOKS LIKE THERE'LL BE NO RUST ON THEM THIS SEASON!

HEY, MIKE, LOOK. THE DYNAMOS GOT THEIR MAN!

SO DID KATE WINDSWEPT. SHE'S DATING ONE OF THEM!

CONCENTRATE, GUYS! RUST REPORTS ARE ON PAGE SEVEN.

DESPITE THE PREVIOUS NIGHT'S TRIUMPH, ELAINE HAD HER DOUBTS.

I'VE BEEN THINKING THAT MAYBE SLIM'S NOT OUR MAN.

ME TOO, ELAINE.

I'D BEEN THINKING ABOUT THE NEXT RO-BALL SEASON AND HOW THE DYNAMOS WERE GOING TO BLOW THE OPPOSITION AWAY!

NOW IT APPEARED I MIGHT HAVE TO START THINKING ABOUT THE CASE AGAIN. STILL, THAT MEANT THINKING ABOUT ROSIE, AND THAT I DIDN'T MIND.

SOMETHING JUST DOESN'T SEEM RIGHT. THE EVIDENCE WAS WAY TOO EASY TO FIND.

YES, AND I DIDN'T GET THE IMPRESSION THAT SLIM WAS THE CRIMINAL TYPE LAST NIGHT.

I THINK WE NEED TO HAVE A LITTLE TALK WITH HIM.

RCPD HEADQUARTERS WERE STARTING TO FEEL MIGHTY FAMILIAR.

MORNING, FELLAS. WHAT CAN I DO FOR YOU?

LIEUTENANT COLE. YOU MIGHT NOT LIKE WHAT I'M GOING TO SAY ABOUT THE CASE.

YOU'RE THINKING THAT IT ALL SEEMED A BIT TOO EASY?

PRECISELY.

LIEUTENANT COLE HAD THE SAME MISGIVINGS ABOUT ARRESTING MELROSE AS MIKE DID, BUT HE WAS KEEPING HIM IN FOR QUESTIONING, AND ALSO FOR HIS OWN SAFETY. IF PEOPLE FOUND OUT THAT THE ROBOT LINKED TO A RUST SCARE WAS FREE AND STILL IN TOWN, HE MIGHT BE SCRAPPED!

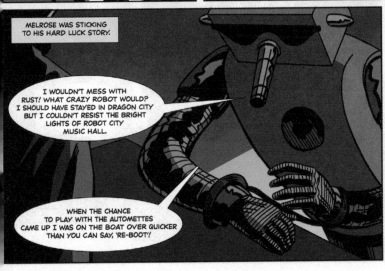

MELROSE WAS STICKING TO HIS HARD LUCK STORY.

I WOULDN'T MESS WITH RUST! WHAT CRAZY ROBOT WOULD? I SHOULD HAVE STAYED IN DRAGON CITY BUT I COULDN'T RESIST THE BRIGHT LIGHTS OF ROBOT CITY MUSIC HALL.

WHEN THE CHANCE TO PLAY WITH THE AUTOMETTES CAME UP I WAS ON THE BOAT OVER QUICKER THAN YOU CAN SAY, 'RE-BOOT'!

BUT EVER SINCE I ARRIVED EVERYTHING'S GONE WRONG FOR ME. THEY EVEN TRIED TO GIVE ME SOMEONE ELSE'S LUGGAGE AT THE DOCKS-- THEY INSISTED IT WAS MINE!

ROD, IT SOUNDS AS IF HE MIGHT BE TELLING THE TRUTH ABOUT THIS LUGGAGE BUSINESS. LET'S GET DOWN TO THE DOCKS AND SEE WHAT WE CAN FIND OUT AT THE SHIPPING LINE OFFICES.

IF SLIM *IS* RESPONSIBLE FOR THE RUST OUTBREAK, MAYBE HE SMUGGLED THE FAKE METAL POLISH IN WITH HIM. I THINK WE SHOULD PUT ON THE OLD DELIVERY-MEN DISGUISES.

DISGUISE TIME. I LOVE IT WHEN WE GO UNDERCOVER-- WE'RE SO GOOD AT IT, SOMETIMES I CAN'T RECOGNISE MYSELF!

THE ROBOT CITY WATERFRONT IS ALWAYS TEEMING WITH LIFE. SHIPS CARRYING ROBOTS, PEOPLE AND CARGO FROM ALL OVER THE WORLD GIVE IT A COSMOPOLITAN FLAVOUR. MIKE AND I BLENDED SEAMLESSLY IN TO THIS VIBRANT SETTING. NO ONE WOULD HAVE GUESSED THAT TWO TOP DETECTIVES WERE IN THEIR MIDST!

HEY, MIKE... ROD! HOW'RE YOU TWO DOING?

HEY, ROD! STILL IN THE INVESTIGATION BUSINESS?

MIKE! ROD! NICE OUTFITS, GUYS!

DON'T ANSWER, ROD. WE'RE UNDERCOVER.

STOP BY FOR SOME PIZZA LATER, FELLAS!

HI, MIKE! HEY, ROD! GOTTA RUN! TELL ELAINE ROBBIE SAYS HELLO.

MAYBE WE'D USED THE OLD DELIVERY-MEN DISGUISES ONE TIME TOO MANY.

ANOTHER SNAG WITH THE DELIVERY-MEN ROUTINE WAS THAT I ALWAYS HAD TO CARRY THE HEAVY PACKAGES.

CAN I PUT THIS BOX DOWN NOW?

NO, ROD. STAY IN CHARACTER. IT'S IMPORTANT TO LIVE THE ROLE!

OK, BUT NEXT TIME I WANT THE CLIPBOARD!

HEY, BUDDY. DO YOU KNOW WHERE I CAN FIND APOLLO SHIPPING LINES?

OH, HI MIKE. SURE, THEY'RE JUST DOWN THERE--THIRD WAREHOUSE ON YOUR LEFT. ARE YOU HERE ON A JOB?

SSSHHH! KEEP IT DOWN-- PRETEND THAT YOU DON'T KNOW ME.

THANKFULLY, AT THE APOLLO SHIPPING LINES' OFFICES WE FOUND THE ONE ROBOT WHO DIDN'T SEEM TO KNOW US.

I WAS GLAD THAT MIKE HAD INSISTED WE STAY IN CHARACTER.

WE'VE JUST GOT TO CHECK ON SOME LUGGAGE THAT ONE OF OUR CLIENTS SAID HE LOST WHEN HE CAME IN ON THE *TIBERIUS* LAST MONTH.

HE WAS A DRAGON-CITY ROBOT BY THE NAME OF MELROSE.

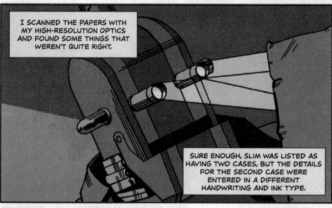

AH, THAT'D BE SLIM THE SAXOPHONE PLAYER, WOULDN'T IT?

DON'T TELL ME HE WANTS HIS OTHER CASE NOW!

YOU KNOW HIM, THEN?

NOT REALLY. BUT I DO REMEMBER HE WOULDN'T COLLECT HIS SECOND CASE OF LUGGAGE. HE MADE A BIG SONG AND DANCE ABOUT IT NOT BEING HIS, AND HE WOULDN'T PAY FOR IT.

LET'S SEE IF I CAN FIND HIS PAPERS. HERE YOU ARE... MELROSE.

I SCANNED THE PAPERS WITH MY HIGH-RESOLUTION OPTICS AND FOUND SOME THINGS THAT WEREN'T QUITE RIGHT.

SURE ENOUGH, SLIM WAS LISTED AS HAVING TWO CASES, BUT THE DETAILS FOR THE SECOND CASE WERE ENTERED IN A DIFFERENT HANDWRITING AND INK TYPE.

LOOK, MIKE. YOU CAN SEE WHERE THE FORM'S BEEN DOCTORED.

GOOD WORK, ROD. AND LOOK HERE. IT SAYS THAT THE SECOND CASE WAS COLLECTED BY DELTA DELIVERIES.

IF YOU GUYS KNOW SLIM, YOU SHOULD TALK TO TONI OUT BACK.

TONI CAME OVER WITH SLIM ON THE *TIBERIUS* AND HAS BEEN TRYING TO GET IN CONTACT WITH HIM.

OK, WE'LL CATCH HIM ON THE WAY OUT.

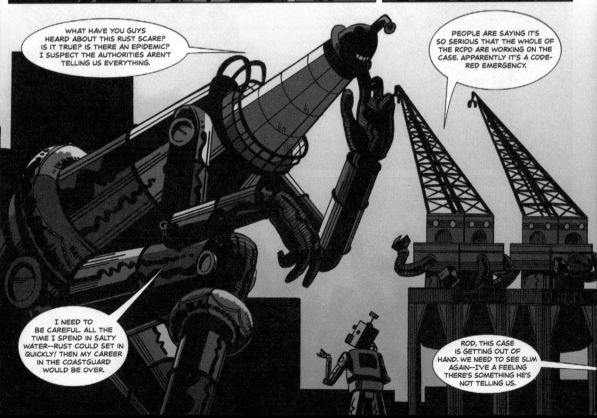

RCPD HEADQUARTERS TWICE IN ONE DAY. IT WAS BEGINNING TO FEEL LIKE I WAS BACK ON THE FORCE.

COME ON, SLIM. WE KNOW YOU HAD A SECOND CASE. WHAT WAS IN IT... FAKE METAL POLISH?

I'VE TOLD YOU I DIDN'T HAVE ANOTHER CASE! WHY DO PEOPLE KEEP ON SAYING I'VE DONE THINGS WHEN I HAVEN'T?

THEY SAID I'D DOWNLOADED ILLEGAL MUSIC SOFTWARE. THEN THEY SAID I HADN'T PAID MY UNION DUES, BUT I'D SENT THEM. I'D PAID EVERY ONE!

SOMEONE'S OUT TO GET ME, AND I DON'T KNOW WHY. THEY EVEN TAMPERED WITH MY SAXOPHONE WHEN I HAD MY BIG BREAK AT ROBOT CITY MUSIC HALL!

AND YOU BLAMED THE AUTOMETTES FOR THAT, DIDN'T YOU, SLIM?!

THE AUTOMETTES? WHA-- NO! THERE'S NO WAY THOSE GIRLS WOULD DO ANYTHING LIKE THAT. THEY WERE ALL VERY SUPPORTIVE. THEY KNEW SOMETHING WAS WRONG BECAUSE THEY'D HEARD ME REHEARSE.

I JUST DON'T UNDERSTAND WHY ALL THIS IS HAPPENING TO ME. I ALWAYS THOUGHT ROBOT CITY WOULD GIVE ROBOTS A FAIR BREAK.

I'D SEEN A LOT OF GUILTY PEOPLE IN MY DAY, AND SLIM JUST DIDN'T SEEM TO FIT THE PROFILE. I WAS BEGINNING TO FEEL SORRY FOR THE GUY. AND I COULD TELL MIKE WAS, TOO.

COME ON, MELROSE. BACK TO THE CELLS WITH YOU.

MIKE. ROD. IT LOOKS LIKE THIS CASE IS STILL OPEN. I THINK MELROSE IS INNOCENT, BUT YOU'VE GOT TO FIND OUT WHAT'S GOING ON BEFORE THIS RUST PANIC GETS OUT OF HAND.

THE WHOLE CITY IS GETTING JITTERY.

AS WE WALKED THROUGH THE STREETS IT SEEMED LIKE BUSINESS AS USUAL, BUT YOU COULD FEEL THE UNDERLYING TENSION.

THE CITY WAS HEADING FOR TROUBLE, AND ONLY WE COULD STOP IT.

YOU THINK SLIM'S BEING FRAMED?

YES. BUT I'VE NO IDEA WHO BY.

RING, RING!

HI, ELAINE. YOU'VE TRACED THE SECOND CASE? GOOD WORK. IT WAS DELIVERED WHERE? A LOCKER IN CENTRAL STATION?

GREAT. WE CAN CATCH THE EL TRAIN AND BE THERE IN FIFTEEN MINUTES.

ROBOT CITY CENTRAL STATION. BUILT IN 1882 ON THE SITE OF THE OLD COTTON MARKET, IT'S GROWN UP WITH THE CITY. YOU'VE PROBABLY SEEN THE MAIN HALL IN THE MOVIES. THEY'RE ALWAYS FILMING SOMETHING HERE.

WE LOCATED THE LUGGAGE LOCKERS ON THE WESTERN SIDE, BY THE SUBURBAN LINE PLATFORMS.

THERE THEY ARE.

LOCKED! STILL, A LITTLE THING LIKE THAT WASN'T GOING TO STOP A ROBOT LIKE ME.

WHAT'S THE POINT IN HAVING POWER-ASSISTED GRIP IF YOU CAN'T USE IT ONCE IN A WHILE?

THERE WAS NO CASE IN THE LOCKER, BUT WE DID FIND...

A GUIDE TO THE THEATRE DISTRICT, SOME OLD FOOD WRAPPERS...

A TICKET FOR LOW'S CHINESE LAUNDRY AND SOME GRANULES OF SALT.

SALT. JUST THE INGREDIENT YOU'D NEED TO START A RUST ATTACK!

WHAT?!

GOOD GRIEF, HAVE YOU HEARD?

WHAT'S THAT? THE EPIDEMIC STARTED AT LOW'S CHINESE?

LOW'S CHINESE, DID YOU SAY? IS THAT THE RESTAURANT ON CENTRAL AVENUE?

HEY--MY FRIEND WORKS NEAR THERE. I HOPE HE'S OK...

I ALWAYS SAID NOODLES WERE A NO-NO WHERE ROBOTS ARE CONCERNED.

GIVE ME A PIZZA ANY DAY.

THIS TICKET IS OUR ONLY LEAD, ROD. HAVE WE EVER DISGUISED OURSELVES AS LAUNDRY WORKERS?

NOPE. THIS IS GOING TO BE A CONFIDENTIAL FIRST!

THE NEXT MORNING.
LOW'S LAUNDRY, RED DRAGON
STREET, CHINATOWN.

LOW'S WAS A SMALL,
FAMILY-RUN LAUNDRY.
ONE OF ELAINE'S
CONTACTS HAD MANAGED
TO GET US SOME SHIFTS
THERE AT SHORT NOTICE.

OVER THE NEXT TWO
DAYS, I GOT PRETTY
GOOD AT IRONING AND
FOLDING. WE FOUND OUT
THAT NO ONE HAD BEEN
IN TO COLLECT THE
LAUNDRY FOR THE
TICKET WE HAD.

SO WE WAITED.
AND WE IRONED.
AND WE FOLDED.

THERE WASN'T MUCH
MORE WE COULD DO,
AS SLIM COULDN'T
GIVE US ANY MORE
INFORMATION ABOUT
THE MISSING CASE.

SO WE WAITED
SOME MORE.

YOU KNOW, THE REASON I
JOINED THE RCPD YEARS
AGO WAS TO HELP CLEAN UP THE
CITY. I JUST NEVER REALISED I'D
HAVE TO DO IT THIS NEATLY.

AT LAST...

PSSST! MIKE!
IT'S OUR GUY! HE'S
PICKING UP SOME...
SEQUINNED DANCE
COSTUMES?!

I'VE LOST MY
TICKET, BUT I THINK
I REMEMBER WHAT
NUMBER IT WAS...

MIKE GESTURED TO ME TO GRAB
A BASKET AND FOLLOW THE ROBOT, AS IF
WE WERE GOING OUT TO MAKE A DELIVERY.

ONE HOUR LATER.
THE AUTOMETTES'
SECRET REHEARSAL
STUDIO.
LOCATION: THAT'S
CONFIDENTIAL!

LADIES.
HOW'S EVERYONE
DOING?

NOT TOO BAD,
THANKS. WE KEEP
COVERED UP WHEN
WE GO OUT, BUT
MAINLY WE STAY
IN THESE DAYS.

SHE'S BEING BRAVE
ABOUT IT. THE ROBOTS
AMONG US ARE HAVING
A TOUGH TIME.

IF YOU DON'T
MIND, WE'D LIKE
TO ASK YOU SOME
QUESTIONS.

OF COURSE.
WE UNDERSTAND.

WE TRACKED A
SUSPECT TO THE DANCE
STUDIO ON GROVE STREET.
ISN'T THAT ONE
OF YOURS?

NOT ANY MORE.
THAT STUDIO WAS
SOLD LAST YEAR TO
WOODGATE HOLDINGS.
IT'S A SHAME, BECAUSE
WE LOVED IT THERE.

YES, THAT PLACE WAS SOLD ABOUT THE SAME TIME LOLA AND HER SISTERS LEFT THE TROUPE.

I MISS LOLA. SHE WAS LOTS OF FUN.

LOLA CRUZ WAS ONE OF YOUR BIGGEST STARS, WASN'T SHE?

THAT'S RIGHT. THERE WAS A RUMOUR SHE WANTED TO SET UP HER OWN DANCE TROUPE, BUT I HAVEN'T HEARD WHETHER SHE EVER DID.

IT WAS SUCH A SHAME. SHE LOVED BEING AN AUTOMETTE, YOU KNOW. AND SHE LEFT SO SUDDENLY THAT WE DIDN'T EVEN HAVE A CHANCE TO SAY GOODBYE.

I HOPE SHE DIDN'T GET RUST.

WHAT CAN YOU TELL US ABOUT SLIM MELROSE?

SLIM? AH, WHAT A ROBOT. SO SOULFUL.

HE WAS A GREAT SAXOPHONE PLAYER AND A REALLY SWEET GUY.

THE NIGHT HE PLAYED HIS BIG SOLO SOMETHING WENT WRONG. I DON'T KNOW WHAT, BUT HE SOUNDED AWFUL. HE SAID SOMEONE HAD TAMPERED WITH HIS SAX.

THEN WE HEARD THAT HE HADN'T PAID HIS UNION FEES, AND THE NEXT THING WE KNEW HE WAS GONE.

YOU KNOW, THINKING THAT YOU TWO ARE OUT THERE TRYING TO HELP US IS ALL THAT'S KEEPING US TOGETHER RIGHT NOW.

THIS RUST... IT MAKES YOU FEEL SO *FRAGILE*. LIKE YOU'RE GOING TO BREAK INTO LITTLE PIECES AND THEY'LL NEVER BE ABLE TO PUT YOU BACK TOGETHER AGAIN.

DON'T WORRY, ROSIE. WE'RE NOT GOING TO LET THAT HAPPEN.

ROD, WATCH OUT. YOUR JAW IS DROPPING OFF AGAIN. DON'T FALL APART IN FRONT OF THE GIRLS.

HOW EMBARRASSING! THANKS, MIKE.

ROD, WE'RE SO GRATEFUL FOR ALL YOU'VE DONE SO FAR.

YOU LOOK AFTER YOURSELF, ROSIE. WE'RE GOING TO CATCH WHOEVER HAS DONE THIS TO YOU.

I THINK ROSIE LIKES HIM, AND I CAN SEE WHY.

CAN YOU REALLY? MUST BE A ROBOT THING...

ONE HOUR LATER.
BACK AT GROVE STREET STUDIOS.

HELLO. WE'RE FROM KELLY HEATING SERVICES.

THERE'VE BEEN SOME PROBLEMS IN THE STREET, AND WE HAVE TO CHECK OUT EVERYONE'S SYSTEMS.

HMM! I HAVEN'T HEARD ABOUT THIS. I'M NOT SURE I SHOULD LET YOU IN.

ALL WE NEED TO DO IS ADJUST SOME OF YOUR RADIATORS. WE'LL ONLY BE A SHORT WHILE.

IF WE DON'T DO IT NOW WE'LL HAVE TO COME BACK TOMORROW.

WE'D LIKE TO CHECK ANY REALLY LARGE ROOMS THAT MIGHT BE DIFFICULT TO HEAT.

OK THEN. I GUESS THE MAIN REHEARSAL ROOM WOULD BE BEST. BUT PLEASE DON'T TALK TO THE DANCERS.

HEY, MIKE. LOOK OVER THERE! ISN'T THAT...

LOLA CRUZ?

THOSE ARE LOLA'S SISTERS AS WELL. SO THIS MUST BE HER NEW DANCE TROUPE.

BUT IT DOESN'T LOOK LIKE SHE'S IN CHARGE...

NO, NO! HOW MANY TIMES MUST WE DO THIS? YOUR FOOTWORK'S ALL WRONG.

AND TURN, AND WAVE... NO! ALL TOGETHER, NOT IN YOUR OWN TIME!

LOLA'S STOPPED. WHAT'S SHE SAYING?

ROD! WATCH YOUR JAW. IT'S GOING AGAIN.

YOU'RE PUSHING US TOO HARD. WE CAN'T CONCENTRATE!

LISTEN, MS CRUZ! YOU MAY HAVE BEEN A BIG STAR AT ROBOT CITY MUSIC HALL, BUT YOU'RE LOOKING PRETTY SLOPPY NOW. WHERE'S YOUR *FOCUS?*

YOU WOULDN'T BE ABLE TO FOCUS IF *YOU* HAD RUST!

THE ONE MAN WE COULDN'T NAIL!

WH–WHAT CAN WE DO FOR YOU TODAY, MR WEST, SIR?

WHAT ON EARTH WAS HE DOING HERE? IT WAS TIME TO LISTEN AND LEARN.

HOW ARE MY WESTERN DOLLS, THEN? ARE THEY READY TO KNOCK THE SPOTS OFF THOSE AUTOMETTES?

THEY'LL GET THERE, BUT I HAVE TO ADMIT IT'S SLOW PROGRESS, SIR. THE AUTOMETTES ARE A TOUGH ACT TO FOLLOW.

WEST WAS ONE OF THE REASONS WE HAD LEFT THE RCPD. HE USED TO RUN A GANG OF CROOKS IN ROBOT CITY. ANOTHER PAIR OF DETECTIVES HAD BEEN KILLED INVESTIGATING HIS ACTIVITIES, BUT WE'D BEEN UNABLE TO PIN ANYTHING ON HIM. HE WAS TOO SLIPPERY BY FAR, AND HAD TOO MANY FRIENDS IN HIGH PLACES, INCLUDING THE FORMER RCPD COMMISSIONER.

MAXWELL WEST WAS THE ONE BLACK MARK ON THE RCPD'S CLEAN RECORD.

DON'T WORRY ABOUT THE AUTOMETTES. I HEAR THEY'VE GOT A TOUCH OF RUST TO COPE WITH.

AND UNLIKE MY WESTERN DOLLS, THEY DON'T HAVE ACCESS TO THE CURE!

MY PLANS FOR ROBOT CITY MUSIC HALL ARE FALLING INTO PLACE, SO I WANT THE WESTERN DOLLS READY FOR A PRESS CONFERENCE NEXT WEEK.

AND REMEMBER– IT DOESN'T PAY TO LET ME DOWN.

ROD, WE HAVE TO FIND OUT WHAT THIS IS ALL ABOUT.

THIS MIGHT INVOLVE SOME REAL HIGH-LEVEL DETECTIVE WORK.

COUNT ME IN.

THIS IS THE ONE. WEST'S OFFICE. CAN YOU GET YOUR RIGHT EAR ON THAT GLASS?

I'M ON IT, MIKE. I CHECKED THE SOFTWARE AND EVERYTHING'S WORKING.

THIS RECORDING WILL BE CRYSTAL CLEAR AND ADMISSIBLE AS EVIDENCE IN A COURT OF LAW.

I'M PICKING UP VOICES. WEST AND HIS MEN HAVE JUST ENTERED THE ROOM.

IN LESS THAN A WEEK THE AUTOMETTES WILL HAVE RUSTED BEYOND REPAIR!

GOOD GRIEF!

THE WESTERN DOLLS WILL VERY CONVENIENTLY FILL THE GAP LEFT BY THEM. THE MERCHANDISING AROUND THE DOLLS WILL MAKE ME A FORTUNE! AND I HAVE AN INGENIOUS PLAN IN PLACE TO ENSURE THAT THE AUTOMETTES' LEGENDARY HOME, ROBOT CITY MUSIC HALL, WILL SOON BE UP FOR SALE. AND GUESS WHO'S BUYING?

I'VE ARRANGED FOR A LITTLE FIRE TO GUT THE MUSIC HALL, AND UNFORTUNATELY, THEY'LL SOON REALISE THAT THEIR INSURANCE RENEWAL HAS BEEN MYSTERIOUSLY 'LOST' IN THE POST. SUCH A SHAME.

THEY'LL BE FORCED TO SELL AFTER THE FIRE-- AT A GREATLY REDUCED PRICE-- AND MY COMPANY WOODGATE HOLDINGS IS POISED TO MAKE A MORE-THAN-GENEROUS OFFER.

IN THIS TUBE I HAVE THE SECRET PLANS FOR THE MUSIC HALL ALL SET OUT. THEY DO NOT LEAVE MY SIGHT. UNDERSTOOD?

YOU TWO LOOK BETTER THAN EVER! LIKE A COUPLE OF MOVIE STARS.

WELL, WE'RE FEELING GOOD ABOUT THINGS. THE AUTOMETTES JUST CONTACTED US, AND WEST'S CURE FOR THE RUST IS BEGINNING TO TAKE EFFECT.

THE RCPD SCIENTISTS HAD TO MODIFY THE FORMULA AS IT WAS A LITTLE UNSTABLE, BUT NOW IT'S WORKING LIKE A DREAM.

SLIM MELROSE WAS JUST AN INNOCENT SCAPEGOAT. WEST'S HENCHMEN OVERHEARD HIM TALKING IN A BAR THE NIGHT BEFORE HE SAILED FOR ROBOT CITY. THEY REALISED THAT, BECAUSE HE WAS GOING TO WORK WITH THE AUTOMETTES, HE WAS A PERFECT TARGET TO FRAME FOR THE RUST ATTACK.

THEY DISGUISED THE CASE CONTAINING THE RUST FORMULA AS LUGGAGE BELONGING TO HIM.

THEN THEY GOT HIM FIRED FROM ROBOT CITY MUSIC HALL TO MAKE IT LOOK AS IF HE HAD A GOOD MOTIVE FOR SABOTAGING THE AUTOMETTES. THEY ALSO PLANTED THE INCRIMINATING EVIDENCE YOU FOUND.

BUT THEY OVERPLAYED THEIR HAND.

I GATHER YOU'RE ALSO CHARGING WEST FOR THE MURDERS OF THE RCPD OFFICERS?

YUP. WEST'S HENCHMAN ARE TALKING, SO WE'LL SOON HAVE ENOUGH EVIDENCE TO NAIL HIM.

I THOUGHT YOU CLOSED THAT CASE, LIEUTENANT?

A CASE IS NEVER CLOSED FOR ME UNTIL I'VE GOT MY MAN. GOOD WORK, GUYS.

I'LL SEE YOU AROUND.

BECAUSE WE'RE A CONFIDENTIAL AGENCY, WE COULDN'T BOAST ABOUT HOW WE'D SAVED THE CITY FROM A RUST EPIDEMIC.

BUT LIEUTENANT COLE LET A FEW PEOPLE IN KEY PLACES KNOW WHO'D DONE WHAT, AND THE PHONE IN OUR OFFICE STARTED RINGING A BIT MORE.

WE STILL LIKE TO GET A LOT OF THINKING DONE, BUT I'VE STARTED GETTING UP EARLIER. LIKE, IN THE ACTUAL MORNING.

MIKE SAID THAT WE SHOULD HAVE A NIGHT OUT TO CELEBRATE, SO THAT'S US IN THE AUDIENCE. THAT'S MIKE AND HIS GIRL. YES, IT'S ELAINE--WHO'D HAVE THOUGHT IT?

AND THAT'S ME ALL DRESSED UP. MY GIRL'S NOT SITTING NEXT TO ME, BUT SHE IS HERE... THIS IS HER BIG NUMBER COMING UP!

THE AUTOMETTES PUT TO REST ANY RUMOURS ABOUT THEIR CONDITION WITH A SENSATIONAL NEW SHOW.

EVERYONE WAS WORRIED THAT AFTER HAVING TAKEN A LONG BREAK FROM PERFORMING THEY MIGHT BE A LITTLE BIT--YOU KNOW--*RUSTY!* BUT THEY'D BEEN REHEARSING. THEY WERE OUT OF THIS WORLD.

THE END